To Isha D.S.

To Lin G.B.

First published in the United States 1991
by Dial Books for Young Readers
A Division of Penguin Books USA Inc.
375 Hudson Street
New York, New York 10014

Published in Great Britain
by Hutchinson Children's Books
Text copyright © 1990 by Dyan Sheldon
Pictures copyright © 1990 by Gary Blythe
Printed in Great Britain
First Edition
1 3 5 7 9 10 8 6 4 2

Library of Congress Cataloging in Publication Data
Sheldon, Dyan.
The whales' song / story by Dyan Sheldon :
paintings by Gary Blythe.
p. cm.
Summary: Enthralled by her grandmother's
story of seeing and hearing whales
singing in the sea long ago, Lilly hopes
to see them herself and to hear their
mysterious songs.
ISBN 0-8037-0972-2
[1. Whales—Fiction. 2. Grandmothers—Fiction.]
I. Blythe, Gary, ill. II. Title.
PZ7.S54144Wh 1991   [E]—dc20   90-46722   CIP   AC

THE WHALES' SONG

by Dyan Sheldon   *paintings by* Gary Blythe

DIAL BOOKS FOR YOUNG READERS *New York*

*L*ILLY'S grandmother told her a story.

"Once upon a time," she said, "the ocean was filled with whales. They were as big as the hills. They were as peaceful as the moon. They were the most wondrous creatures you could ever imagine."

*L*ILLY climbed onto her grandmother's lap.

"I used to sit at the end of the pier and listen for whales," said Lilly's grandmother. "Sometimes I'd sit there all day and all night. Then suddenly I'd see them coming toward me from miles away. They moved through the water as if they were dancing."

"*B*UT why did they swim to you, Grandma?" asked Lilly. "How did they know you were there?"

Lilly's grandmother smiled. "Oh, you had to bring them something special. A perfect shell. Or a beautiful stone. And if they liked you, the whales would take your gift and give you something in return."

"WHAT would they give you, Grandma?" asked Lilly. "What did you get from the whales?"

Lilly's grandmother sighed. "Once or twice," she whispered, "once or twice, I heard them sing."

*L*ILLY's great-uncle Frederick stomped into the room. "That's nothing but a silly old tale!" he snapped. "Whales were important for their meat, and for their bones, and for their blubber. If you have to tell Lilly about whales, then tell her something useful. Don't fill her head with nonsense. Singing whales, indeed!"

"THERE were whales here millions of years before there were ships, or cities, or even cave dwellers," continued Lilly's grandmother. "People used to say they were magical."

"People used to eat them and boil them down for oil!" grumbled Lilly's great-uncle Frederick. And he stomped back out of the room.

*L*ILLY dreamt
about whales.

    *In her dreams she
saw them, as large as
mountains and bluer than
the sky. In her dreams she
heard them singing, their
voices like the wind.
In her dreams they leapt
from the water and called
her name.*

*I*n the morning Lilly went down to the ocean, to the place where no one fished or swam or sailed. She walked to the end of the old pier. The water was empty and still. She took a yellow flower out of her pocket and dropped it in the water.

"This is for you," she called into the air.

*L*ILLY sat at the end of the pier and waited.

She waited all morning and all afternoon.

Then, as dusk began to fall, Uncle Frederick came down the hill after her. "Enough of this foolishness," he said. "Come on home. You can't be dreaming your life away."

*T*HAT night Lilly awoke suddenly.

The room was bright with moonlight. She sat up and listened. The house was quiet. Lilly climbed out of bed and went to the window. She could hear something in the distance, on the far side of the hill.

*S*HE raced outside
and down to the shore.
Her heart was pounding
as she reached the sea.

There, enormous in the
ocean, were the whales.

They leapt and jumped
and spun across the moon.

Their singing filled
the night.

Lilly saw her yellow
flower dancing on
the spray.

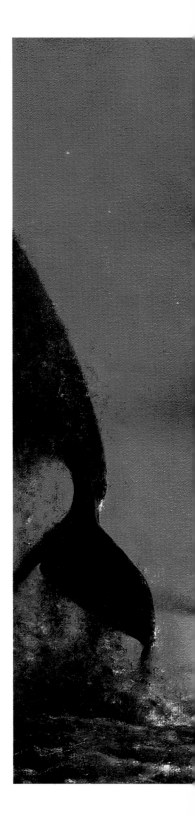

MINUTES passed, or maybe hours. Suddenly Lilly felt the breeze rustle her nightgown and the cold nip at her toes. She shivered and rubbed her eyes. Then it seemed the ocean was still again and the night dark and silent.

Lilly thought she must have been dreaming. She stood up and turned toward home. Then from far, far away, on the breath of the wind, she heard

"Lilly!

Lilly!"

The whales were calling her name.

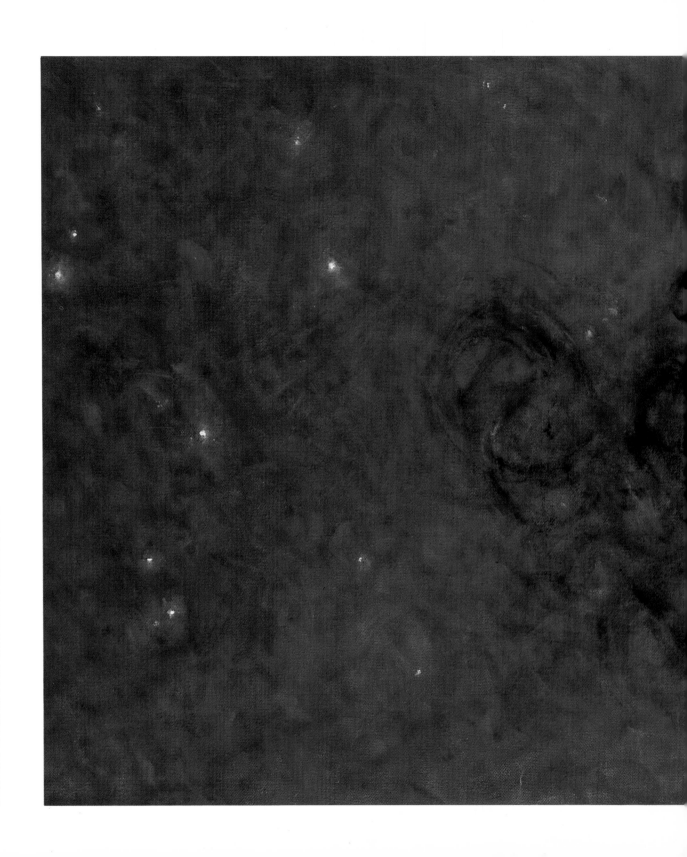